Night
Wings

The Black Circle
Chronicles – Book 3

GARY LEE VINCENT

Burning Bulb
PUBLISHING

Night Wings
By **Gary Lee Vincent**

Burning Bulb Publishing
P.O. Box 4721
Bridgeport, WV 26330-4721
United States of America
www.BurningBulbPublishing.com

Cover concept by Gary Lee Vincent with photos from KHIUS from Shutterstock, Erik McLean from Pexels, Dg fotografo from Pexels, and Amit Talwar from Pexels.

First Edition.

Paperback Edition ISBN: 978-1-948278-38-6

Printed in the United States of America

DEDICATION

To my band of misfits at Burning Bulb Publishing,
who are blind to the impossible, impervious to the
opinions of the naysayers, and continuously strive to
bring exciting stories to life.
I love you all.

CHAPTER 1

"Oh no, not those damned birds again," Timothy Lowe, gardener and handyman at the Wickenburg, Arizona branch of the Joy of Life Bible Church remarked angrily to himself as he stared at the large black bird sitting on top of the wall opposite him.

It was early summer and old Timothy had been gardening along happily until the bird showed up. But now, he stopped digging the patch of earth where he intended to plant a seedling, straightened up his wiry body and leaned on the handle of his shovel.

As though it had been waiting for him to do this, the bird let out a loud squawk: "Ca-ca-cawww!"

Timothy winced in mental agony. He'd forgotten how bad their noise was—the cawing sound they made filled his old head with a shrill ringing similar to the sound of ball bearings rolling around in a metal pail.

"Ca-ca-cawwww!"

"Sweet Jesus! Stop that godawful racket," Timothy howled at the bird when he couldn't stand it any longer. Then he grabbed up his shovel and advanced threateningly on it.

The bird flew off, over the church building. Following its flight with his eyes, Timothy didn't think it had left the church premises, but it didn't make any more noise, and out of earshot was just fine with him too.

He was unable to get back to work though. The bird's sudden reappearance bothered him immensely. He hadn't seen one of them for three weeks, not since the night that sister Wendy Wilson had died during a prayer meeting intended to cast the devil out of her. Timothy shuddered. He didn't like remembering that night.

There had been no doubt at all in his mind that sister Wendy had somehow gotten possessed by the devil. Pastor Fisher had attempted to engage the demon inside her in conversation and as a result words had begun forming on the church wall. In all of Timothy's years as a born-again Christian he'd never seen anything like that. It had been crazy, like watching a movie.

The large black words had dripped down the church wall while threatening havoc against the church. And then suddenly, Wendy Wilson had gasped; and her neck had begun lengthening and had twisted and cracked.

Because Wendy had died from a broken neck, there had been an autopsy, and the police had questioned everyone who had been present at the scene of her death. So that the police didn't think they were all crazy, Pastor Fisher had cautioned them not the mention the writing on the wall to anyone, but they'd told the detectives all the rest. The police had thought they were all crazy anyway.

But the coroner's report had removed any suspicion of foul play by the church members.

According to the coroner, the vertebrae in Wendy's neck had not just been broken—they'd been shattered into little pieces as if hit by a twenty-pound sledgehammer. The problem with this though, was that there were no bruises or other signs of trauma at all on her neck—no injuries to her skin or muscles—that might have accounted for such violent damage to her spine. At the very least, given the pulverized state of its vertebrae, her neck should have looked like a chunk of hamburger patty.

On hearing that, the police had filed Wendy Wilson's death as 'Inexplicable' and had released her body for burial.

The whole church had been at Wendy's funeral and morale amongst the members had since been at an all-time low.

Timothy scowled now as another of the nasty black birds flew past the church. He heaved a loud sigh of relief when it chose not to land on the compound's wall but kept on going.

The thing was, that since Wendy's death, the birds all seemed to have vanished.

And something else had happened on the night that Wendy Wilson died, something that Timothy Lowe hadn't told anyone, not even his daughter Becky.

Before they'd begun praying for Wendy that night, one of the black birds had been perched on a branch of a low tree outside the auditorium. They'd all noticed it, but Pastor Fisher had decided that the bird had had nothing to do with the evil afflicting sister Wendy.

Timothy had initially thought so too. But...during their prayers, he'd glanced again at the window and had seen that the black bird had shifted its position. Now it was sitting on the windowsill and was staring in at them intently. Indeed, it had almost seemed as distressed as Wendy was. He'd been about to point out the winged creature's strange behavior to the pastor when the giant words had begun appearing on the church wall.

Then, in the horror that had followed, Timothy had completely forgotten about the bird. Until the next day that was. About to trim the hedges that bordered the west wall of the church auditorium, he'd come across the bird again. This time though, it was lying flat on its side on the west-side walkway and was stiff with rigor mortis.

The dead bird's mouth had been open, with a thin stream of blood running from it onto the concrete flooring. But weirdest of all had been that when Timothy picked the bird up—the first time he'd even had physical contact with one of them—its neck had lolled sideways in a way that contradicted its frozen state.

When Timothy had felt the dead bird's neck, it had been as flexible as if every bone in it had been pulverized to powder. He'd been confused then; but had decided to bury the dead creature without telling anyone about the strange nature of its death. He'd interred it in a corner of the churchyard and afterwards forgotten about it...until the coroner's report on the impossibility of the injuries to Wendy Wilson's neck had come in.

The similarities between the two deaths—avian and human—had chilled Timothy to the core. But he'd decided to keep quiet about it. Pastor Fisher had already rejected any question of the black birds being involved in the spiritual conflicts currently affecting and afflicting their small town of Wickenburg, Arizona in general and the Joy of Life Bible Church in particular, and Timothy Lowe saw no point in ruffling anyone's feathers.

But now, watching as the same black bird which had earlier flown past the wall of the church compound (or another member of the same repugnant species) flew past him again, this time headed in the opposite direction, Timothy Lowe couldn't help but feel very worried.

Those damn things left when Wendy died. And now they're back again. Good Lord, what do they want this time!?

***

"Brother Timothy?...Brother Timothy?"

So deep in thought was the old church gardener cum handyman that it took a few seconds before he realized that he was the one being addressed.

Then he turned to see who was speaking to him. Assistant pastor Josh Davies, a young, dark-haired man in his early thirties, was peering at him with a concerned expression on his face.

"Oh, brother Josh. I'm sorry I didn't hear you," Timothy said, trying to shrug off the chill that he felt despite the warm of this midsummer day.

"I'm looking for Mrs. Fisher, the pastor's wife. I wondered if maybe she'd strolled around this way."

Timothy shook his head. "Haven't seen her around here. Maybe she went to fetch something from the parsonage."

Pastor Josh nodded. "Maybe you're right. I'll go look for her over..." Then his previous look of concern returned. "But...you looked really worried about something, brother Timothy. Is anything the matter?"

Timothy shook his head. "No, sir, I'm just fine. Just remembering a death, that's all." Timothy's sense of unease and foreboding wasn't something he could explain to anyone, especially not a newcomer to the church.

Josh Davies and his wife Connie had been transferred to Wickenburg from Tucson a week ago on special request from Pastor Fisher, who hadn't been himself since Wendy Wilson's death. The young couple were to serve as assistant pastors and also as evangelists, with the mother church in Tucson hoping that their arrival here would boost the congregation's flagging morale and also stir up church growth. Timothy liked the pair of them, but he had the feeling that this new guy also wouldn't welcome any talk of possessed birds afflicting the church.

So, he just smiled. "Ah, don't mind me, brother. I just get ta thinkin' like this sometimes."

Josh peered at him some more and then nodded. "Well if you say so, sir. I'll just get a move on and look for Mrs. Fisher then." Then he nodded at the wall around the church yard. "What species of bird is that, brother Timothy?"

Timothy looked at the bird and sighed and shook his head. "I don't know. They're a nuisance and a pain and if it wasn't for the love of Jesus and the fact that this place is the church of God, I'd take to bringing a shotgun to work every day just to shoot 'em!"

The way Josh stared at him told Timothy that maybe he'd said too much. "Don't mind my ranting, son. I'm an old man now and the noise those things make is just too much for my old ears."

Josh nodded. "Yes, I've heard them; they do make a horrible racket. My wife can't stand them either." Then he grinned. "Hey, maybe we can put down poisoned bait to kill the ones that visit the church. That might discourage the others from hanging around here. I'll mention it to the pastor."

The idea of poisoning the birds hadn't occurred to old Timothy. "Sir, I'll be in your debt if you do that. There's something really creepy about this species."

"Anyway, I gotta get a move on," Josh said. "See you later, sir."

Timothy watched him walk off and smiled: *Yeah, poisoning those birds is a great idea.*

Then he looked over at the bird perched on the wall again, and winced when it let off another raucous squawk: "Ca-ca-ccaaaaw!"

CHAPTER 2

"His behavior was extremely odd," Josh told Connie that night on the drive home from the Joy of Life Bible Church, recounting the afternoon's discussion with the church gardener. "The old man just stood there staring into space and didn't hear me until the third time I spoke to him. I'm not exaggerating when I say he looked spooked by something."

Connie, a small and pretty blonde, nodded understandingly. "What a nice little town this is," she said as her husband turned their car onto Mesa Drive, where they lived.

Josh nodded too. "But if even half of what Frank Everett told us is true, this appearance is extremely deceptive."

"I know, honey. But just look at this place. From outward appearances, it's impossible to believe that Wickenburg is in as much of a spiritual mess as brother Frank and Pastor Fisher claim it is."

"I agree...but..."

"But what, darling?"

Josh turned the car into their driveway. "Well, honey, I can't say for sure that what had gotten brother Timothy spooked like that had to do with this town, but that's partly the feeling I got while talking to him."

"Hmm, now that's worrisome," Connie replied as Josh parked. "We'll really need to pray about that."

"Yes," Josh readily agreed, getting out of their car and looking up at the darkening skies. "I really wish I knew what the problem is with this town."

***

"I did discuss the birds with Pastor Fisher, but he was wholly against the idea of poisoning them," Josh said during dinner.

Connie looked up in amusement from her plate of spaghetti and meatballs. "He did? And why's that? We're not talking of killing off the whole species here, just the few that fly into the church grounds. They are a real nuisance."

Josh shrugged. "His argument is that we need to be wary of the birds not dying on the church premises but flying off and dying somewhere else where kids might find their bodies....I sort of reason along with him there: the Joy of Life church is enough in the doldrums without a host of 'criminal negligence' lawsuits to deal with."

"Yes, I see what you mean," Connie agreed. "Still, we could try to trap them then."

Josh shook his head. "He's against that too. His first argument is that trapping them will likely be in violation of some state or county animal rights stipulation or the other—he's possibly right in that— and his second argument is the same reason he doesn't want us poisoning the birds: kids. We set the traps and some kid just might sneak out of the kindergarten section during church service and go stick his hand in one. Or possibly worse, find a live but wounded bird in a trap and try to let it out. And those birds look really mean. Pastor Fisher said he could just imagine a kid without eyes."

"I must admit that he's got some good points," Connie said with a laugh. "It does look as though we're stuck with the little devils for the foreseeable future."

Little devils? Josh mused on that bothersome term through the rest of their dinner.

CHAPTER 3

"Them? Here? I don't believe it," Karen Houston said on recognizing the couple reflected in her crystal ball. The crystal ball sat on the coffee table in her living room, its base resting on circular black cloth embroidered with astrological symbols.

Karen had been using the crystal ball to monitor happenings at the Joy of Life Bible Church through the eyes of one of her black bird 'familiars,' and now she summoned her brother over to come a have a look also. "Hey, Bill, come see who's just arrived in town."

"Huh?" Bill Houston—bald, dark complected, and heavily tattooed put down the book of magic spells he was reading and shifted chairs to sit beside his sister. The image in the crystal ball wasn't exactly HD-quality, but he could clearly see the couple it showed standing on the front steps of the Joy of Life church auditorium; and he had no doubts as to their identities.

At first Bill frowned on recognizing Josh and Connie Davies, but then he burst out laughing, slapping his hands on his thighs in his mirth. "Oh heck, li'l sis, if it ain't your old ex and his prude girlfriend!"

Karen, who didn't look so much like her brother as she did a sensual, voluptuous vixen—long black hair, sapphire blue eyes—plus some tattoos; that much she did have in common with Bill—made a face as if she'd swallowed something horrible. "I don't see what's so funny about it," she objected. "We've a huge score to settle with Josh and Connie, and..." Her lips twisted into a frown as she noticed the wedding rings the couple both wore. "Hey, Bill!—she's not his girlfriend anymore. They're married now."

Bill squinted to notice the couple's hands in the tablet-sized image in the crystal ball. It wasn't easy, but he shortly saw the wedding rings too.

"Well, it'll make it sweeter to destroy their marriage then, won't it?"

On hearing that Karen began grinning.

***

Bill and Karen Houston's mission in Wickenburg was a simple one: to destroy the Joy of Life Bible Church. The siblings were members of an organization called the Black Circle, an organization which had only one aim: to put an end to Christianity.

And for whatever reason, the Black Circle wanted the little town of Wickenburg for themselves. Neither Bill nor Karen knew what exactly it was that made Wickenburg so desirable to their superiors. They had tried to find out but weren't high up enough in the Black Circle hierarchy to be granted access to such privileged information.

Bill and Karen didn't care though. The pair both hated Christianity with a passion, and going beyond mere hatred, they also found great fun in destroying the lives of the followers of God Almighty.

It was during one such mission to destroy the Joy of Life church in Tucson, Arizona that Bill and Karen had encountered Josh and Connie Davies. The couple had been unmarried then and but for the grace of God had almost fallen victims to the Houston's plans.

Sure, God had won that time, but Bill and Karen didn't intend to let Him win again.

This mission in Wickenburg was too important to screw up for any reason. The objective was simple: finalize the clearing of all the churches out of the town. There had originally been eighteen churches in Wickenburg. By their persistent oppression and persecution of the faithful, and the manufacturing and manipulation of scandals, including driving a number of well-known Christian ministers to suicide or seducing them into adultery or fraud, the Black Circle had, over the past four years, successfully shut down seventeen of those eighteen churches, and scattered their congregations like sheep without a shepherd.

All that stood in the way of their owning the town of Wickenburg now was the Joy of Life Bible Church. Several attempts had been made to shut down the Joy of Life church, but for some reason it always bounced back. Which was, of course, completely unacceptable to the Black Circle.

And so, Bill and Karen Houston, brought in to Wickenburg at this final stage of the church-BC conflict, were determined to bring this church too to ruin, to destroy it just like all the others before it.

***

"We gotta maintain our focus," Bill told his sister as the image in the crystal ball clouded over until the ball was merely a glass sphere again.

She looked at him seriously. "What do you mean, Billy? We've got to teach those two a lesson, show them they can't trifle with our magic powers."

Bill scratched his long, black goatee under chin and nodded. "Yeah, yeah, I know how you feel. Still, I'm thinking, we mustn't get distracted from our main mission here. Sure, I'd also like to make those two pay big-time for the embarrassment they caused us in Tucson....But...here's the thing: what we're here to do is much too big to let our personal feelings play a part in." He pointed to the crystal ball. "We don't want to take a chance on what we're setting up failing just 'cos we wanna settle old scores with those two."

"They both attend the Joy of Life church," Karen said. "We may be able to kill two birds with one stone."

"I love the way you put that," Bill said. "Two birds—one stone."

Karen got up and walked over to the living room windows and pulled the drapes wide apart. She remained there staring up at the darkening sky. "This shouldn't be too difficult," she said, lowering her gaze until her eyes were focused on the little house across the road on their right. "You know I can easily find out from Becky what Josh and Connie's role in the church is."

"Okay," Bill cautiously agreed. "We'll try to get them too. But..." he made a warning gesture with his index finger, "only so long as it doesn't interfere with our primary objective. We're at such a critical point now that just about anything could ruin it."

Karen turned around to look at him. "Don't worry, I'll be very careful. I too understand how delicate things are now."

CHAPTER 4

Timothy Lowe was washing up the dishes after dinner, but his mind wasn't really on the task. His thoughts kept going to his daughter Becky, who was outside chatting with her new friend Karen, the girl who lived across the road.

The kitchen door was situated at an angle to the living room, so Timothy couldn't see the two young women, and also his hearing wasn't as good as it had been, so he couldn't hear what they were discussing either, but their loud laughter reached him loud and clear.

It was partly Becky's happiness now that bothered Timothy. *I just wish she was like this all the time.*

A bitter feeling came over Timothy's soul as he soaped the dishes. He got like this sometimes.

The kitchen cooking range was too high now for Becky to reach in her wheelchair and so Timothy did all of their cooking and the washing up; tasks that he didn't mind doing in the least, though Becky sometimes claimed that being unable to help out in the kitchen made her feel useless.

Another burst of joyful laughter came from the living room. The bitterness in Timothy's soul remained firmly in place. This was one of those times when he felt angry at God for letting his daughter have the car accident that had paralyzed her from the waist down.

No, Lord, he thought. *No, I'm not sayin' You were supposed to condone her sins or whatever...but, Lord, You could've at least considered me, her father, that I'm an old man and I can't really cope with a wheelchair-bound daughter, not considering my workload at the church.*

But of course, God didn't seem to have heard him. This was largely the case nowadays and Timothy had no idea if he was the one losing faith because of his misfortunes, or if it was that God simply couldn't be bothered about him anymore.

Or maybe he never was bothered about me in the first place. Maybe I've spent most of my life believing a lie—Jesus and the saints and all that.

Timothy froze in shock at the horrible thought. *Now why the hell would I think like that? I've been a Christian most of my adult life and always told others about God's goodness and—*

"Ca-ca-caw!"

A loud squawk from one of those horrible black birds that were everywhere nowadays cut short his grim thoughts. He looked outside and saw the bird, sitting on a tree branch and looking in at him. After cringing and grimacing at the damned creature's unholy noise, he tried to regain his train of thought.

"Ca-ca-cawww!" This noise came from another bird somewhere out of sight.

Timothy felt like he was losing his mind. "Oh, dear God Almighty, if You really give a damn about me, please stop this god-awful racket."

But as if God was confirming to Timothy that He didn't care about him, the racket continued, with the birds squawking at one another as though they were holding a conference about how to drive Timothy crazy.

Timothy finally abandoned doing the dishes and staggered out of the kitchen. He was relieved that the birds suddenly stopped making their noise.

When Timothy arrived in the living room, Karen was leaning forward on the couch and was gesturing at Becky, who was listening with an intent look on her face, while one of her hands rearranged her red hair.

Karen was saying, "Yeah, girl, I know it sounds real crazy, but I don't think it's any crazier than that faith healing you Christians practice. And you do claim that works. Well, this works too."

The young women hadn't yet noticed Timothy, and he paused, half to get his wits about him again after the black birds' aural assault on his sanity, and also to eavesdrop on their conversation.

"I don't know," Becky replied Karen, gesturing to her crippled lower body, but with an eager look in her eyes. "You just said it's not foolproof."

Karen smiled sadly at Becky and then lowered her voice to an almost-whisper as if she didn't want Timothy (who was supposedly still in the kitchen) overhearing. "I just don't wanna raise your hopes, that's all. But that said, at the moment, you're bound in a wheelchair anyway? What have you got to lose?"

"My salvation?" Becky protested. "I'm a Christian, God doesn't approve of our consorting with idols."

Karen was about reply to that, when Timothy, who suddenly felt unable to remain where he was for much longer without slumping to the floor, sighed loudly and alerted them both to his presence. Karen immediately clammed up with a guilty look on her face as if she'd been caught stealing, and both young women warily watched Timothy approach them.

"Are you okay, dad?" Becky asked as Timothy lowered himself into an armchair.

"Yes, you really look strained," Karen said.

"I think you're overworking yourself at the church," Becky said, steering her motorized wheelchair over to his side and placing a hand against his forehead. "I really think it's time you maybe reduced your workload with them to a part-time job." She peered inquisitively at him. "We can do that now that I'm working again."

"No, no, it's okay," Timothy protested weakly, smiling to reassure the two young women.

Maybe Becky's right, he thought. *Maybe it's just the strain of work—tending flowerbeds and fixing things all day long that's getting to me. I ain't young anymore. Maybe it's time I gave it a rest.*

Becky had recently resumed work at the same high school where she'd taught before her accident. She no longer taught history though but had been put in charge of school records and administration. She mostly worked from home now, and only had to be at the high school premises twice a week.

"I'll try to bring over a relaxing herbal potion for you next time I come," Karen said, joining Becky by her father's side. "I wish I'd thought of this earlier, but it's too late now; the potion takes about two hours to make."

"Thanks." Timothy nodded and smiled at the young 'witch,' as he still thought of her. She looked so strange in his 'Christian home,' with her black satin dress, black fingernails and the cabalistic tattoos that decorated both her arms and her neck.

But looks don't really show a person's heart, Timothy thought. *Despite not being a Christian, Karen's a good girl and means well.*

At the moment, until Becky's wheelchair-accessible van arrived, Karen was the one who drove Becky to the high school when she needed to go there. The pair had recently become very friendly and even went shopping at the mall together.

Timothy's main reservation about their friendship had been that 'Light should have no communion with Darkness,' but now he questioned that reasoning.

Does God even care that we're down here?

Staring into Karen's eyes, he found it strange that he'd ever really believed the Bible.

"You two young ladies were discussing somethin' when I got here," he said to divert them from discussing his health. "What was it?"

Karen immediately looked at Becky in alarm. "Er...nothing, Mr. Lowe. We were just—"

But then Becky interrupted her, saying: "No, it wasn't nothing, daddy. She was telling me about an ancient ritual that—if done correctly—would let me walk again."

"I didn't say it *would* work," Karen objected. "I said *it might* work."

"Well, it's better than nothing," Becky objected in turn. "All I do at the moment is wait for God to do a miracle and heal me, a miracle that I know will never happen, no matter how long I pray and have faith."

And then tears began pouring from her eyes.

Timothy didn't know what to say. At another time he might have told her, "Hey, girl, faith means we gotta trust in God and believe He hears us even in our darkest situations," but now, he felt dry and empty himself, hardly able to speak.

Staring at Becky's miserable face, the tears rolling down her cheeks, he felt himself about to weep too. He was relieved when Becky spun her wheelchair around and headed it towards her bedroom.

"Oh, my God, what have I done?" Karen gasped as her friend rolled away from them. Then she apologized to Timothy: "I'm really, really sorry I mentioned it," she told him.

Timothy gestured in the direction of Becky's bedroom. "Go talk to her for me, wilya? Please ensure she doesn't harm herself again."

An alarmed look came over Karen's face. Timothy knew she was remembering Becky's attempt to commit suicide after she'd first gotten paralyzed.

"Oh, my God no!" Karen gasped and rushed off after Becky.

Timothy stared up at the ceiling and groaned. "No, God, You really haven't been looking out for me for all these years, have ya? This all just gets worse and worse and worse by the day!"

But Timothy really had no idea how bad things were going to get.

As if in agreement with the old man's statement, a black bird crowed somewhere in the distance.

CHAPTER 5

After seeming to innocently mention a cure to Becky Lowe, Karen and Bill waited patiently for a response. In the interim Karen magically fed images of wellness into Becky's subconscious mind, along with a desperation to achieve a cure for her paraplegia by any means necessary.

Although Timothy Lowe and his crippled daughter had no way of knowing it, Karen had been seeding rebellion against Christ in his and his daughter's mind for over a fortnight, ever since she and Becky's supposed 'friendship' had begun.

The Devil is very patient. And most Christians have a weakness somewhere—it could be just about anything, not necessarily a sin; but everyone has something that troubles them, something that the Devil can use as leverage against them.

Because God truly does work in mysterious ways, and sometimes He take ages to respond to the requests of his children; while the Devil, even if he tends to be rather unreliable and prone to give one a scorpion in place of an egg and a snake in place of a fish, seems generally much quicker to respond to his worshippers' requests for his assistance, and many times finds an opportunity to deceive the Christian faithful into believing that his solution to their problems is to be preferred to petitioning the Creator of the universe.

So, Karen and Bill Houston waited.

And they didn't really have to wait too long. Three evenings later, Timothy Lowe was seated in their living room.

"You've really gotta help me out," the old man said. "I've really no one else to turn to now."

"It's Becky, isn't it?" Karen asked softly, trying to sound sympathetic and not show how pleased she was that everything was working out exactly how her brother had planned.

The old man nodded his gray head. "Yeah, she's gotten obsessed about that healing spell or ritual that you told her about. She simply won't give it a rest anymore." He sighed and then looked accusingly at Karen. "But you said you'd talk her out of it."

"I tried to," Karen lied. "While driving her to the school, I explained how it was all very dangerous and told her she'd be better off doing the sensible thing and praying for God's intervention instead." Of course, Karen had done no such thing. What she'd really done was assure Becky that, yes, there was a good chance of the ritual working, but that she was equally certain her father would never stand for her participating in it. And then she'd sworn Becky to silence.

"But you're church folk," Bill told Timothy. "Why not discuss it with the pastor?"

Timothy Lowe rolled his eyes. "Pastor Fisher is out of town, and I don't trust these new pair of assistants of his in the least."

"Oh, you mean Josh and Connie Davies," Bill said.

"You know 'em?" Timothy asked, and then once Bill nodded, went on, "Yeah, that's the pair of 'em. Can't stand the brats and I dunno why. I used to like 'em both, thought they were good people, but then their real character seemed to bubble to the surface, and I can just tell that they're hypocrites."

Bill and Karen nodded sympathetically. What had actually happened was that Karen had cast a spell of enmity between Timothy and the Davieses.

"Anyway," Timothy went on, "the pastor's out of town at the moment and now Becky's begun acting up that this is all my fault, and how she's gonna kill herself if I don't let her have a shot at walking again." He scowled. "God must really hate me, huh?"

"It ain't that bad, sir," Bill said soothingly. "If she wants us to perform the ritual, we can do that."

Timothy looked at Karen, who nodded. "Yes, we can perform it. But like I already told her, there's no guarantee of it succeeding."

"That's fine by me," Timothy said with relief. "Just so long as she gets her blasted ritual. At the moment I'm scared to go to work 'cos I don't know if she'll still be alive when I return home."

"Sir, there is the issue of payment to consider," Bill said. "No, no, not monetary payment," he added quickly, on seeing the look of wariness that came into Timothy's eyes. "But...well, sir, it's like this: if the ritual does work and your daughter can walk again...well, if that happens, then both your soul and hers then belong to our dark master and you'll be expected to join our organization, the Black Circle and work with us to achieve our aims."

Timothy looked bemused for a few seconds, but then he nodded grimly at the siblings. "Yeah, yeah, that's fine with me. The way I see it now, God doesn't care a bit about me, and so why should I bother myself with caring what He wants, huh?"

Then, as he understood the full implications of what Bill had just said, his eyes widened and he asked, "Huh, d'you mean that the ritual actually might work? That Becky really might walk again?"

Karen laughed. "Well, as you Christians always say—God works in mysterious ways. And I can assure you, sir, so does the Devil." She glanced over at her brother and then added, "Go home now, sir and tell Becky that we'll hold the ritual in your home tomorrow night at midnight."

Timothy Lowe nodded and rose to leave. "Thank you both very much. You're serious though? Becky really might walk again?"

Bill nodded. "If we perform it right, there a huge chance that she will. At the very least she'll stop hounding you and threatening to off herself."

Timothy nodded and scratched his brow. "Yeah, that'll be a huge relief. At the moment she sounds worse than those damned black birds that are everywhere in town."

They all laughed at his comment and then the old man left and crossed the road to his home and his crippled daughter.

When he'd gone, Bill winked at Karen. "Game on, li'l sis."

She grinned back. "I dare say. And I dare anyone to stop the powers of Hell from winning this time."

CHAPTER 6

The ritual was conducted on schedule at midnight. All four of them were present in the Lowe's living room, with Becky seated on the floor with her back propped against the couch.

I can't really believe I'm doing this, Timothy Lowe thought as he watched Karen and Bill unroll a large red rug decorated with a black pentagram out over his own carpet. *I'm actually permitting a satanic mass to be held in my house. Even a year ago such a happening would be impossible; I'd have run the devil worshippers out of my driveway, with a shotgun if available; but now I'm one of them!*

Timothy tried to imagine the scene if by some freak happening, one of the members of the Joy of Life church walked in now and saw what his living room looked like—curtains all drawn and all the lights off; the room instead illuminated by a forest of lit red and black candles in gothic candlesticks. He and his Becky both wore long black robes with attached hoods, satanic surplices borrowed from the Houstons, who were similarly dressed.

Rather than feel disgusted at himself however, Timothy felt a thrill of anticipation. He looked over at Becky. She was clearly excited too, but was tempering her joy at having gotten her way with reservations over the outcome of the night's activities.

Timothy understood the cautiously optimistic look in her eyes: *Of course, she's thinking, what if the ritual don't work? If that's the case, then she'll be going from a major high to a crushing low.*

Karen and Bill finally got things arranged to their satisfaction. They set up black candles at the five point of the pentagram on the rug and then turned to stare in turn from Becky to Timothy. Their pale faces looked ghostly in the wavering candlelight.

"Now remember this," Karen told them both. "If this ritual works and Becky does get back her ability to walk, the souls of both of you then belong to the Devil. You will become one with us and will help us achieve our aims and purposes in this town." She paused and then asked: "Do you both agree to this?"

Becky instantly nodded, and Karen looked at Timothy expectantly.

"Only if it works?" Timothy asked. "Why's that?"

Karen smiled an eerie smile within the confines of her hood. "My father the Devil is nothing like how you Christians portray him. You have a choice in what happens here. Unlike the God you're used to, you're under no obligation to worship Lucifer if he fails to convince you of his power."

"But if he does," Bill added with a grim smile, "then you must renounce all others as God and bow before Satan alone. What possible excuse could you have not to do so, once he's shown you how great he is?"

"Say yes, dad," Becky told him in a pleading voice. "We've already discussed this."

"Yes," Timothy agreed. "If your master—your 'father' as you call him—can raise my daughter from her bed of infirmity, I will serve him and no other."

Bill stared directly into his eyes and he looked back without flinching. "Yes, let's do this," he told the younger man.

"Good," Bill said. "Give me a hand with moving Becky onto the pentagram."

Timothy and Bill lifted Becky and positioned her in the pentagram with her arms spread sideways, so that from where he stood her body formed a sort of inverted cross.

"Now we need blood," Karen said, stepping up to Becky and then bending over her with a ceremonial knife in one hand and a ritual chalice in the other.

Becky, already schooled in the basics of tonight's ritual by Karen, quickly took the knife from her and, while still lying on her back, fearlessly sliced open her left palm. Karen collected the resulting spill of blood in the chalice and stepped back. Becky laid her arms in their original position again, seemingly heedless of the blood that now trickled from her wound onto the red cloth.

Karen gestured to Bill and Timothy. "Kneel, both of you. Kneel before our master Satan!"

Timothy knelt, as did both Karen and Bill. Karen began chanting. The words weren't English, although every now and then Timothy though he heard her mention 'Satan' and 'Becky' and 'healing.'

And then suddenly, the room began to change. The furniture stayed the same, as did the relative positions of the four of them to those solid objects. The room, however, seemed to become less solid, less real.

But what surprised Timothy the most was the impression he had that the four of them were no longer alone in his altered living room. He could clearly make out black transparent shapes—actual shapes, not shadows—amidst the gloom cast by the candlelight. And the shapes were those of huge birds. Timothy also thought he understood of what sort those birds were.

Oh, my God! So this is the source of—

But he had no time to think the rest of it, because something else was happening and that thing took his mind off of the bird shapes and focused his attention on his daughter, who lay with her eyes wide open and staring and expectant, and on Karen, who still knelt beside her.

This time Karen's words were in English. "Come to me, dark master of Hell's flames! Heed my supplication and demonstrate your power by healing this one!"

Looking beyond Karen, Timothy saw a portal open in the darkness, a wavering ghostly door. Karen threw the blood in the chalice at the opening and it all vanished, was sucked away out of sight. And then, almost too fast for the eyes to track, something came flying out of the portal in return, something that seemed both to have lots of wings and to be liquid also. This ectoplasm settled over Becky and while she struggled to breathe, it sank down into her body.

"What in the world just happened?" Timothy Lowe muttered under his breath. But his question was answered when Becky, still spluttering like she was being ducked underwater, began kicking her legs.

And while Timothy gaped in shock, Karen stood up and pulled Becky up onto her feet also.

"How do you feel?" she asked Becky.

But Becky was crying tears of joy and unable to reply.

Next, the room began to normalize again. It solidified while the giant bird shapes faded. The portal from which the healing ectoplasm had come faded too, until there was nothing where it had been except the home entertainment system.

"Oh, I'm healed," Becky finally gasped, flinging back her black hood. "Thank God!"

"Not God," Karen gently corrected her. "Satan. Always thank Satan for his blessings from now on."

Becky nodded. "I'm sorry I forgot. Thank Satan!"

Timothy smiled and went to embrace his daughter. For the shortest of moments, he had a sudden doubt about the rightness of what they'd just done here. But a single look at the delight on Becky's face convinced him that he'd made the right decision.

God didn't answer me; but the Devil did. I wonder what else Satan can do for us?

"There is one last part of the ritual," Karen told them both when they had extinguished the candles and turned the living room lights back on. Then she handed both Timothy and Becky a necklace with an amulet shaped like a black bird.

"Both of you must wear this at all times," she said. "It's both a symbol of your dedication to the Darkness and a way for you to channel your new powers."

"Powers?" Timothy and Becky both stared at the Houstons. "New powers?"

"Yeah," Bill said with a grin. "The Devil hasn't just healed Becky, he's also granted you both the ability to make changes to your environment."

"I don't understand," Timothy said, accepting one of the necklaces from Karen and draping it around his neck. What sort of powers are you talkin' about?"

Becky had already put on the other necklace. And at the moment she seemed too delighted to care about any new powers that she might have; she was striding back and forth around the living room, bending down and straightening up and making short abrupt runs.

"Oh, I'll explain later," Bill said. "But for the moment, the first thing you're gonna do is pretend that Becky ain't healed yet."

"Yeah, we wanna give the credit for this miracle to the church," Karen said.

Becky stopped her pacing. "Why's that?" she asked with a broad smile on her face. "Oh, I just love Satan so much now that I'll do anything he asks me to, including torching the nearest church and its entire congregation. But I'm curious as to why you want to go this route and give God the credit for healing me."

Karen explained: "This way it'll be an even bigger blow later when the truth comes out."

"So, what you do, Becky," Bill said. "Is you stay in your wheelchair until Sunday morning, and then, during Pastor Fisher's sermon, you leap up and praise the Lord for healing you. Or better yet, you go forward for prayer, if there's an altar call for those who want to be healed and then you leap up out of your wheelchair and start singing and weeping and thanking God."

"Just remember to give the credit for your healing to God, not to Satan," Karen said, to which they all laughed.

And right at that exact moment, the black birds outside Timothy Lowes's house began making their loud racket again. Only strangely, this time Timothy didn't find their noise offensive in the least. In fact, now he found the cawing noises the black birds made wonderfully soothing, almost as calming as a chorus of lullabies intended to lull him to sleep.

CHAPTER 7

When Becky Lowe got up from her wheelchair that Sunday morning, the Joy of Life church indeed erupted into pandemonium.

"Oh yes, folks, praise the Lord!" Pastor Amos Fisher enthused, after attempting to calm the congregation for the third time and failing. "Praise Jesus. Praise God Almighty on high."

The people kept dancing and praising God and the two church musicians, a drummer and a keyboard player, played on and on and on until everyone was sweating and almost delirious with joy, with the 'healed' girl and her father dancing and singing more vigorously than anyone else.

"Oh, praise our glorious Savior, our dear sweet Lord Jesus!" Pastor Fisher said breathlessly when he finally managed to quiet the conversation down. "You know, I really didn't intend to pray for the sick today, but I just had a witness in my heart to do so. I just had a divine stirring—that incredible feeling that a miracle was gonna take place the moment I placed my hands on our dear sister Rebecca Lowe to receive her healing. Oh, my dear God, you truly are glorious. Yes, brothers and sisters, you've no idea how overjoyed I am. Our brother here"—he gestured to Timothy and Becky Lowe to ascend the steps to the altar platform,—"brother Timothy has been a faithful servant in the Lord's vineyard for years and he truly deserves God's blessing in this manner."

"Preach it, pastor!"

"Yeah sir, preach it!"

"Brethren, if our faithful brother here did not get this miracle, then who would? I tell ya, folks, this just goes to show that we should never cease praying. No, we should never cease trusting in God." Pastor Fisher embraced the weeping father and daughter, and then added. "Yes, brethren, we gotta be faithful to God 'cos he's always faithful to us."

Then he handed the microphone over to Becky. "Share your testimony with the church, sister Rebecca. Let everyone know what great things God has done for you!"

Becky Lowe took the microphone from the pastor, and weeping, said, "I'm just so overwhelmed. Oh, thank you, Jesus! I just don't know what to say...!"

***

Although as surprised as everyone else in the church that Sunday morning, Josh Davies felt troubled too. Something just didn't 'feel right' about this miracle he'd just witnessed happening. Josh did feel happy for Becky, but...

What is wrong with me? he thought in confusion. *Why do I feel like this? There's no chance here that she was faking; everyone in this church—no, not just this church; possibly everyone in this part of town— knows that she broke her back and was told she'd never walk again. But...*

Josh didn't get it. Becky was still weeping and hugging her father and leaping up and down; and the church was still full of rapturous applause; and this miracle was clearly the work of Jesus and this was going to bring a great increase in the church membership; but despite knowing all of this, Josh felt like he'd swallowed a large stone.

He looked right, at his wife Connie who was seated next to him, along with the other officiating ministers.

Connie was clapping her hands like everyone else. She turned to Josh with a huge smile on her face. "Oh, this is just great, darling. Praise God, and now we're surely going to see an increase in the church attendance. I'll be surprised if this doesn't trigger off a revival in town even. It'll be fantastic to get the doors of some of the shut-down churches to open up again!"

Josh nodded and tried to smile.

Maybe I'm just being silly. This is a genuine miracle and I should accept it as such and not—

But then his eyes strayed to the windows, and he saw the large number of black birds sitting on the church's surrounding wall. And what Josh found even more disconcerting than the number of birds was how quiet they all were.

I'm definitely going to pray about this, Josh told himself. *Maybe I feel bothered because this miracle is going to trigger another onslaught of spiritual attacks against the church.*

CHAPTER 8

Becky Lowe whistled as she walked down the street. Being out of her wheelchair felt so good. She had to restrain herself from skipping from sheer joy.

It was the Tuesday evening after her supposed healing at the Joy of Life Bible Church and Becky was on her way to buy groceries.

She'd become an overnight celebrity in the little town of Wickenburg. Now everyone wanted to know her again. Pastor Fisher was even trying to get the local newspaper to cover her story, but so far, he hadn't had any success.

"Ca-ca-caww!"

Becky turned and waved at the black bird that now followed her everywhere. At the same time, she unconsciously fingered her bird-shaped amulet. The bird had just landed on a tree ahead of her and was watching her with inquisitive eyes. Its gaze was questioning; expectant.

Becky understood what the bird wanted. It wanted her to send it on an errand of some kind.

"Your bird familiars will do whatever you tell them to," Karen had explained to Becky and her father after her healing. "Within reasonable limits, of course."

"Yes, I'm powerful now," Becky thought, but she'd not yet made the bird do anything for her. She was still so happy merely to be able to walk again.

Becky grinned at the bird and kept walking. She found it strange how easily people could be deceived. *No one at all suspects that it wasn't God who healed me, but the Devil. Oh, thank you Satan!*

She paused at an intersection and waited for the 'Walk' light to turn. An old woman whom she knew—Mrs. Roper—was walking towards her on the other side of the road.

On noticing Mrs. Roper, Becky suddenly felt mean. An intense and totally uncharacteristic desire to hurt the old woman came over her.

Becky looked around until she found her dark familiar perched on a roadside fence, then she nodded at the bird and whispered, "Get her, boy! Get the old crone!"

That was all it apparently took to get results.

On her command the bird launched itself across the road like a missile, swooping up and over a passing car to reach its target.

Mrs. Roper never knew what hit her, but suddenly she was upended and flailing in midair, with her shopping bags flying everywhere. Then she crash-landed into the main road, with her fall causing several cars to swerve across into the opposite lane to avoid hitting her.

Wow! Becky was impressed with the results of her simple command. She felt immensely powerful and a deep satisfaction filled her. Her black bird was seated up in a tree in the front yard of the house beside where Mrs. Roper had had her misfortune, looking completely innocent of the crime; and now that Becky thought back on what had happened, she realized that she hadn't actually seen the bird hit her victim.

And this is eerily similar to how I had my own accident. When my truck crashed I both felt and saw birds attacking me, but afterwards it appeared that I'd just hallucinated it all.

Mrs. Roper's accident now caused a traffic holdup, with several drivers stopping to render assistance to her. The 'Walk' light came on now and Becky crossed the road too. When she arrived besides Mrs. Roper, she saw that the old woman was both alive and conscious, but that her left leg was broken just below the knee, with white bone visible in the wound.

Becky turned away from the forming crowd and smiled. Then, feeling another surge of power pass through her, she continued on her journey to the grocery store.

She was due in a new converts' class in the church in about an hour. She wondered what wonderful things her new powers would permit her to do there.

***

During the new converts' class, Becky sat on a rear pew which afforded her a clear view of both her bird familiar and the church members. She bowed her head for the meeting's opening prayer but of course she didn't pray. She no longer had any faith in Jesus at all. But because of her 'miracle healing' she was now a celebrity in the church and everyone loved seeing her there.

She spent most of the meeting causing trouble. This was ridiculously easy to do: she would whisper an instruction to the bird and then secretly point a finger at someone or nod her head towards the person, and the next thing that would happen was that that person would start showing signs of discomfort. For instance, she kept making sister Juanita, who was teaching them all, cough. Then she told the bird "Ants" and nodded at brother Carl, who immediately started scratching his thighs as if something was crawling on them and biting him. Then sister Helen suddenly yelped that a wasp had stung her; but of course, there was no wasp anywhere in sight.

Becky had great fun for a while, but she went too far when she extended the 'itching treatment' to sister Juanita. On realizing that she was itching for no reason at all, this devout Latino lady put two and two together and suddenly yelled out loud:

"Okay, enough! You evil spirits disrupting this prayer meeting, in the name of Jesus I order you to vamoose! Be gone in Jesus' name!"

On that command, a very strange thing happened to Becky. A chilled feeling enveloped her body and just like that, she discovered that she could no longer move her limbs. She felt terrified and would have screamed, but her mouth was frozen too, set in the smile she'd had on her face when sister Juanita had begun itching.

A quick glance out of the window as the chill was settling on her had shown her her bird familiar suddenly jerk violently as if it had been shot or hit by lightning and then fall off its perch and out of sight.

And so, frozen on her seat was how Becky Lowe spent the next hour-and-a-half of the new converts' teaching class, with no one any the wiser to her plight. Everyone else was just delighted that the demonic distractions had ceased.

All the time that Becky sat there motionless, she was scared that she had both lost her demonic healing and had now become quadriplegic to boot. Her terrifying paralysis only lifted after sister Juanita said the prayer to close the meeting.

After that Becky couldn't leave the church premises fast enough.

Never again, never again! she vowed as she hurried back home. She'd felt true terror in the church that night, fear of the power of God that she'd not experienced when she'd been a good girl.

Then she remembered her black bird friend and how it had been similarly stricken and had fallen from its perch. Was it dead? She looked up at the sky and the trees to see if it was accompanying her. It wasn't up there. Where was it?

Finally, she did locate the bird. Yes, it was once more following behind her, although now it was hopping after her on the sidewalk, like it was too tired to fly.

"Okay, so we're both allergic to Jesus now," Becky said. "I gotta keep that in mind."

Instead of turning into her house, she crossed the road to visit Bill and Karen and question them about what had just happened to her.

CHAPTER 9

Just like his daughter Becky, Timothy Lowe had also begun discovering the dubious benefits of worshipping the Devil. In his case though, he hadn't yet hurt anyone physically, he mostly used his powers to strengthen himself at work; having that extra burst of energy made all the digging and raking up he had to do much easier.

Old Timothy straightened up from tending a flowerbed and leaned on the head of his shovel. One of the black birds was flying past the church and he lifted a hand and waved at it. The birds no longer bothered him at all. In fact, the sight of one of them filled him with a dark joy.

He was very pleased with his and Becky's new family situation. He was also amazed at how everything in his life had been changed for the better by that one simple decision that he'd taken, his choice to do what was best for his daughter and damn the consequences.

"Hello, brother Timothy. It's such a lovely day, isn't it, sir?"

Timothy controlled himself as he turned towards the hated voice.

Nowadays he really couldn't stand either Connie Davies or her husband Josh, but seeing as the young couple were his bosses, he had no choice but to be civil to them.

Connie was smiling at him, but Timothy nonetheless felt a deep surge of hatred burn through him. He felt mad enough at Connie Davies to split her head in two with his shovel.

"Oh hello, sister Connie," he said through gritted teeth.

Connie clearly didn't notice his ill temper. "Oh, what lovely flowers," she enthused in delight. "You really have a flair for this!"

"Just time and practice, sister. Nothing that you and Pastor Josh couldn't develop yourselves given time." He laughed. "But of course, you two are always occupied with preaching the Gospel of our glorious Lord and Savior."

There was heavy sarcasm in his tone, but Connie just nodded and breathed in deep, inhaling the smell of the blossoms into her lungs. Then she grinned at him. "Well, I gotta go now," she said. "Josh and I need to drive into Tucson, to pick up some ministry supplies from the church headquarters there."

She turned to walk away from him, then seemed to remember something, because she suddenly turned back again.

"Oh, sorry I forgot to mention it. We seem to have a leak in the roof of one of the counseling rooms."

"Which one of 'em?" Timothy asked, all the while wishing he could wrap a bit of his hose around her neck and choke her to death.

Connie turned and gestured in the vague direction of the administrative block, which was invisible from where they stood because it was situated on the other side of the church building. "It's the one right at the end of the hall; the large one where the drama group hold their rehearsals. Last night when it was raining, water was streaming down the walls."

"I'll have look at it." Timothy indicated his dug-up flowerbed. "Can't do it today though. The pastor's insistent that he wants more flowers everywhere."

"Oh, the flowers are just great," Connie said again, leaning forward and taking in another huge sniff of their fragrance.

Timothy watched her walk off around the front of the church. Once again, he was filled with that deep rage, that almost senseless desire to harm and maim her in some way.

So now you're ordering me around, huh? I really gotta teach you and that husband of yours a lesson. Just you wait and see if I don't!

His unreasoning anger at Connie only vanished once she'd vanished from sight. And then Timothy once more leaned on his shovel, his mood ruined for the morning. He huffed and puffed for a while and then gripped the amulet dangling inside his faded overalls and grimaced.

Last night Bill and Karen had given Timothy the task of ruining the Davies's marriage.

Scowling, Timothy figured it was time he got to work doing so. Timothy had been assigned the job because he worked in the church with couple, meaning he was around them all day long. The birds would help him accomplish his evil end, but Timothy had to focus the birds on their targets.

And now, gripping the bird amulet hard, Timothy told the birds exactly what he wanted them to do.

***

Josh turned the starter key again in the ignition. Still the car wouldn't start. After a fifth try, he stared at his wife in confusion. "I don't get it. It ran okay this morning." Then he glanced at the fuel gauge and saw that the tank was empty.

Josh found that funny: *Hey, I thought Connie filled the tank yesterday. It was full this morning...or wasn't it?*

Josh figured his memory was playing tricks on him. He turned to Connie, who was sitting beside him in the front passenger seat. "Looks like we aren't leaving here until we put some gas in the tank."

"But I filled the tank yesterday," Connie instantly protested in surprise. "What happened to the gas I bought!?"

"Are you certain you filled the tank?" Josh asked, irritation building in him.

"Of course I did, darling. Don't you believe me?"

"Of course I believe you, honey," Josh replied, then gestured to the fuel gauge. "But if you *did* fill the tank with gas, where is it now?"

He's blaming you, a soft voice whispered in Connie's mind.

"Hey, don't blame me," Connie instantly replied Josh in a heated voice. "All I know is that I bought gas in the car tank yesterday when I went to the store."

She's lying, a similar small voice whispered in Josh's mind, skillfully mingling itself with his thoughts so it sounded like his own opinion. *She forgot to fill the tank yesterday and now she's pretending innocence.* Neither he nor Connie had noticed the two black birds perched on top of a nearby car.

Earlier, while Josh and Connie were inside the parsonage, Timothy Lowe siphoned gas from their car and used it to fill the church's lawncare equipment. Now, on Timothy Lowe's instructions, the birds were magically engaged in stirring up an argument between them.

Josh said, "Well, I'm not calling you a liar, honey, but—"

He IS calling you a liar, the bird told Connie. *And you're definitely not going to take such insinuations from him!*

"Hey, I don't have to sit here and listen to this," Connie said suddenly, pushing the front passenger door open.

"Listen," Josh said, trying to keep his own temper under control, "all I'm saying is that you maybe forgot to fill the tank. It's no big deal. Not something to lie about."

You see? He does think you're lying. He thinks you spent the gas money on clothes or shoes! Why would he think that? Aren't you both Christians? You've never lied to him before now? Why would you lie about something as insignificant as gasoline?

"Stop it, stop it, stop it! I'm not lying! Why would I lie to you!?" Connie yelled at Josh and slammed the car door. Then she stomped off back towards the church offices.

Josh watched her go, thinking for the first time since their marriage that maybe, just maybe, he'd married the wrong woman.

The birds helped his thoughts along. And, peaking at the couple around the side of the church auditorium, Timothy Lowe had a good laugh at their anguish.

**

Their argument was clearly a foolish one and by half an hour later Connie and Josh had already apologized to each other and made up. Neither of them was any longer in the mood to motor down to Tucson today, so they sat in their office looking through some paperwork that Pastor Fisher needed reviewed.

Seeing a further opportunity to cause mischief between them, Timothy quickly dispatched the birds to their office.

After they'd been reviewing files for a while, Connie passed Josh a printed design update for the flyers to promote the church's women's retreat scheduled for October. "Have a look at this, darling. Something seems wrong about the colors."

"Okay, honey, I'll look it over in a moment. Just gotta tally up these figures again."

The black birds moved in then, making Josh completely forget her request. He didn't remember that he was supposed to check the artwork for the flyers until Connie tapped him on his shoulders.

"Have you looked at it yet?" she asked.

"Huh?" Then Josh remembered what she'd asked him to do. But then came the thought: *Why does she have to be so dependent on me for every little thing?*

"I haven't the time to look at it now," he said brusquely, pushing the flyer back at her without looking at her. "You decide if you like it or not."

The birds were already working on Connie too: *See, he doesn't care about you. You really did marry the wrong man.*

"I thought you loved me, Josh? Don't you even care about me enough to assist me when I'm stuck?" Connie asked him.

Josh looked up now, demon-bird-fuelled irritation written on his face. "Darling, what are you talking about? I've got half the work and you've got the other half. I haven't asked you to help me out with anything, have I?"

She's really pathetic, the birds told Josh. *What did you ever see in her? You had that hot babe Karen Houston, who really loved you; and you dumped her for this?*

He's just another loser, the birds told Connie. *Your friends warned you about him, but you didn't listen.*

"I don't know why I ever married you," Connie told Josh. "You're such an insensitive pig...you don't know the first thing about love or a woman's feelings."

"What the...?" Josh began, anger almost boiling over in him now along with a feeling of violence that he'd never felt before. He found himself looking around their office for something to throw; to throw at the walls, throw at the floor, or even throw at Connie herself.

For her part, Connie, her mind boiling over with thoughts that weren't her own, burst into tears.

"What's the matter with you now?" Josh demanded in a loud voice.

"You're just a pig!" Connie yelled at him and then ran outside, looking for somewhere private to weep.

Outside Josh could hear Timothy Lowe laughing as if he was joking with someone. *Dude, I wish I could be as happy as you right now*, Josh thought.

But then he felt bothered, because it sounded as if he heard birds laughing along with old brother Timothy.

But Josh let it go, deciding he was hearing things. At the moment he was still too angry with Connie to think clearly about the possible spiritual implications of what he'd just heard.

***

It's just as well that there normally aren't many of us here during work hours, Josh thought when Connie hadn't returned after ten minutes. *Otherwise, we'd really have been putting on a 'bad Christian' show for them today.*

Aside from himself and Connie, the only others who worked at the church office were Pastor Amos Fisher and his wife Madge, Timothy Lowe (who was always busy fixing something or other around the grounds), and Frank Everett, the church administrator. Frank was currently over in the neighboring town of Prescott helping set up a new branch of the Joy of Life church there, and as Frank had also been overseeing this church's prayer group, Connie was filling in for him on the intercession front.

By now Josh's state of mind had begun returning to normal, and while still angry at Connie for the vaguest of reasons, he'd also begun rationally questioning the reasons for his anger.

Okay, so she forgot to fill up the car tank yesterday, and...but Connie never lies to me, so...or did somebody empty our tank?

That question couldn't be answered. *But even if she did lie to me—no, she didn't—yes, I know she didn't...but even if she did lie, why did I flare up like that?*

She doesn't care about you, the birds whispered. *Man, you made a world-class mistake in marrying her. And God hates divorce. Oh boy, what in the world are you gonna do now?*

Just as at the two previous times, these thoughts presented themselves in Josh's mind as if they were his own. But this time, with Connie not present to focus his anger on, he realized what was going on:

This is the Devil speaking to me!

And once that occurred to him, everything made sense. *Connie and I haven't argued like this since we got married, so why now, all of a sudden?*

However, if Josh didn't know the reason for their unusual marital conflict today, he definitely knew the solution. He quickly opened his Bible to Matthew 18:18 and read it out aloud in the silence of the office: "Devil, the scripture says that whatsoever I shall bind on earth shall be bound in heaven, and whatsoever I shall loose on Earth shall be loosed in Heaven. Satan, in the name of Jesus, I order you to leave me and my wife alone. Every demonic force attacking my marriage, I rebuke you now in the name of Jesus and I command you to leave me and Connie alone!"

After uttering this spiritual command, Josh felt waves of calm pour over him, like soothing balm to his soul. He smiled, understanding in that moment that he had gotten the victory for both Connie and himself.

Oh, my God, where is she? I'd better go make up with her. Oh, how I hate the Devil!

With that thought in mind he quickly departed his office to go look for his wife.

***

"Are you sure you're alright?"

"Oh, it's nothing," Timothy Lowe grunted to Connie as he tried working some feeling back into his right arm. "It happens occasionally," he lied. "But then after a few minutes it clears up. I've got some pills for it at home."

Connie nodded but looked unconvinced. "You don't look too good," she said. "Maybe you should take a break; or even call it quits for today."

Timothy, who was in intense pain but was struggling not to let her realize it, shook his head. "No, no, I'll be fine in a few minutes."

Timothy just wanted Connie to leave him alone. Her presence seemed to be increasing his agony. She had no idea what the real problem was, and he couldn't tell her either.

What had happened was, that Timothy had heard Josh shout, "In the name of Jesus!" and at that exact moment it had felt as if an invisible bolt of lightning had struck him. His right arm seemed to have taken the brunt of the attack; at first it had felt paralyzed but now it had the worst case of pins-and-needles that he'd ever suffered in his life.

"Okay, if you say you're okay," Connie said. "But if you need to go home, just...hey, what happened to those birds?"

Timothy looked where she indicated and saw what she meant. Two of the black birds lay on their backs with their legs stuck up in the air. One of the birds was clearly dead, the other one died while they watched it, letting out a weak caw that sounded like a plea for mercy.

"Ugh," Connie said, her mouth twisting up in disgust. "I really hate those things."

"Don't worry, I'll get rid of them." Timothy felt saddened by the birds' deaths. But of course, he couldn't say that.

"Connie, darling!"

Timothy was very relieved when Connie left him alone and ran off to her husband's side. He was very displeased to see the couple kiss and make up and then depart happily for their office again.

It looked like all of his hard work this afternoon had been for nothing.

"But," he said aloud. "If at first you don't succeed..."

Grimacing from the agonizing pain shooting up and down his right arm, Timothy began digging a deep hole to bury the dead birds in.

CHAPTER 10

"It's just a minor setback," Karen told Timothy that evening, while rubbing a magical salve onto his hurt right arm. "Happens occasionally, nothing to worry about." The salve made Timothy's arm tingle, but the arm also immediately felt much better and Timothy was grateful for the relief.

"But I didn't expect that," he protested meekly. "I thought you said our master is stronger than theirs."

"Of course, Satan is stronger," Bill confirmed from across the room, waving his bottle of beer at Timothy. "And don't you dare doubt it, sir. 'Cos unlike the Christian Jesus, Satan ain't very forgiving."

"Our dark lord doesn't really tolerate failure," Karen said.

Timothy gulped and nodded. "It wasn't my fault," he said nervously. "Everything was going great—I heard them arguing with one another—until that damned fool began casting out the demons in the name of Jesus. And that's when the birds died too."

"Like I said, it happens sometimes," Karen told him. "But we never quit. We prowl about like lions seeking prey. And there is always juicy Christian prey to devour."

"Just don't screw up again," Bill added. "One never knows when the Master might need a scapegoat and decide to make an example of someone."

CHAPTER 11

Becky didn't leave the house for two days after the church debacle. She simply did not feel up to it, so she stayed home and worked at her high school job. The school had already heard of her miraculous healing and were making plans to bring her back to work full-time, but they needed to find her a new post, as her original teaching position had since been filled.

At about noon on Thursday, however, Becky grew tired of all the clerical work she was doing on her computer and decided to take a walk to the grocery store. She intended to pick up some chicken for dinner and also some beer. Now that she was no longer dedicated to Jesus she had begun drinking again. In fact, last night she had gotten so drunk she'd been unable to see straight. Which was of course because she'd finished all of the remaining alcohol in the house.

But at the moment Becky really did feel a need to get out of the house. So, she got up from her computer, put on some street clothes, and picked up her purse.

Once outside, she looked around for her bird familiar. The bird was once more perched up on a tree branch and seemed totally recovered from its shock at the church.

"Come on, dude, we're going shopping," Becky told it in a jaunty voice and started walking down the driveway.

The bird beat its wings, preparatory to taking flight, but then Becky stopped it with the gesture.

"Shush!" she told it and then stared coldly right, across her fence at her neighbor's front yard.

Her neighbor Mark Wilson was outside mowing his lawn. Becky did not know why Mark was at home at this time on a Thursday, but that was not the matter uppermost in her mind.

All she could think of now was how much she hated Mark. Her intense hatred of him filled her in a rush and was accompanied by a collage of images of the blissful time they'd shared together as lovers; and also by the memories of how, after suffering the accident which had crippled her, Mark had then ditched her and gone back to his wife Wendy.

For a moment, concealed behind the tree in which the bird sat so that she could watch Mark without him knowing she was observing him, Becky was taken aback by the sheer intensity of her bad feelings for her ex-lover.

Yes, she knew she was not being entirely fair to him.

Both of us suffered tragedies, though not at the same time.

Mark's wife Wendy had died barely a month after Becky's accident and Mark hadn't been the same since. *Which is probably why he's at home now mowing his lawn and not at work.*

But this calm and logical appraisal of their joint tragedies didn't last long.

Let's get him! He deserves to be taught a lesson for what he did to you! The violent thoughts filled Becky's mind like a storm of scared birds scattering before an intruder. Startled by their vehemence, she looked up at her black bird and it seemed to be nodding "Yes, let's do it" at her.

Across the fence, Mark had taken a break from his task and was mopping his brow with a handkerchief, while the lawn mower sputtered and growled like an angry lion.

When Mark turned to stare in Becky's direction, she quickly ducked out of sight behind the tree.

Oh yes, I'm going to get even with you, you unfaithful bastard!

After this decision it was merely a question of deciding *what* to do to Mark. Already knowing her bird's capacities, she tried to think of something spectacular.

Should I have the bird make his lawn mower malfunction and maybe chew his leg up?

It was a tempting idea, but on reconsidering it, she didn't think it went far enough.

Or maybe I should have the bird break both of his legs...or his back. That's it, I'll put him in a wheelchair too, so he'll know exactly how I felt.

But even this somehow seemed too little a thing to do to Mark, who now, in Becky's angry mind seemed to have committed the sin above all other sins.

She glanced across the street at the Houston's place. *Now what would Karen do in a situation like this?*

She wished she could ask Karen, who was certain to be home at the moment. But if she got her phone out of her purse to call her dark mentor, Mark was certain to hear her calling and then she would lose the element of surprise. Mark might even engage her in conversation, and at the moment she had no desire to speak to him.

Oh, how Becky hated him then!

But then, with her gaze moving back across the road from Karen's house, she saw a car coming. The vehicle was a large blue Toyota SUV with two laughing men in it; something that would certainly do a lot of harm to Mark.

"Do it!" the madness shrilled in her mind. And she, a mere pawn to her anger, similarly shrieked at the bird, "Do it!" pointing at the car and then nodding towards the unsuspecting Mark Wilson.

Mark looked up in surprise at her yelling, but probably mistook it for the bird's loud squawking. The black bird was already in flight and it seemed to vanish in mid-air.

And next, the blue Toyota SUV, which had just reached Mark's front yard, lost control, skidded up over the sidewalk, and crashed through Mark's fence and plowed across his lawn towards him.

Mark had no chance at all. He stood there as if paralyzed, and the SUV mowed him down as if he was a blade of grass, while the driver fought a futile battle to control his runaway car.

And then there was blood on the lawn, and Mark was nowhere to be seen, and the blue SUV, which had amazingly seemed to speed up in the short time since it left the road, crashed into the front of Mark's house.

"Oh, my God, no!" Becky screamed, as both the car and the front of Mark's house now burst into flame.

Struck by a sudden impulse, Becky looked back across the road towards the Houston's place. Karen was standing at her living room window and seemed to be laughing uproariously.

Becky collapsed to her knees on the grass and she covered her ears against the pathetic screams coming from the men dying in the car.

Oh, my God, I've just murdered three people, she thought in horror, gazing over her fence at the flaming car and house, over which her bird familiar was flying at low altitude.

The bird's evil delight at the carnage it had caused came to her like the heat from the flames, but all Becky felt was horror and intense regret.

"Oh, God, help me! What have I become!?" she wept aloud.

CHAPTER 12

Two hours later, Becky was at the Joy of Life Bible Church, seated in Pastor Fisher's office.

She would have come here earlier, but the intervening time had been spent in giving descriptions of the tragedy to the firemen (after they'd put the blaze out), and the police, who had of course wanted to know exactly how the accident had occurred.

Becky had told them exactly what she had seen, but of course she had left out her own involvement in it; not that they would have believed her anyway. The law could not prosecute supernatural criminals.

Ever since causing the fatal accident Becky had been unable to stop weeping.

She had been there, watching across her fence, as the coroner's office had collected the three incinerated bodies, and those images seemed burned into her brain now.

Most important of all, Becky could not forgive herself. She doubted if she would ever be able to do so.

Causing Mrs. Roper's accident had seemed a little thing—that broken leg was something that the old girl would recover from in time—and all the mischievous stuff she'd done in church had just been fun and games. But this?

What had just happened went beyond all of Becky's comprehension.

What scared her the most was how she'd seemed to completely lose control of herself when the rage had come over here. Yes, she did understand and accept that she'd wanted to punish Mark, but he didn't deserve to die.

It wasn't as if he had hurt me that badly.

But no, that was the thing here...Thinking back as calmly as she could manage, and running her mind over the individual details of the incident, Becky clearly remembered how her rage had both started and had then begun to spiral up and away, till it had wound up well out of her control. It had seemed as if someone else had momentarily taken control of her...

As if she had merely been a vessel to fulfill someone else's diabolical plans.

NO! I'm not a murderess! she'd screamed in her mind.

Then she had looked up into the tree where the black bird was perched. The creature had a piece of flesh in its mouth which she hoped didn't come from one of the victims.

"Don't'cha worry 'bout it," Karen had said soothingly. "Mistakes like this happen sometimes when one uses one's powers."

Karen had emerged from her house just before the fire truck arrived. And despite her sounding shocked later on, on first observing the burning house and car from up close, the woman had had a pleased smirk on her face, a disgusting expression of depraved satisfaction which had instantly reminded Becky of the similar look of delight on Karen's face when she'd earlier been staring through the window of her bungalow.

I wonder, Becky had thought, *did Karen take control of me just now and use me to do her will?*

Seeing as how the Joy of Life Bible Church was on the same street as Becky's house, it had been no surprise to her when her father had shown up; the smoke from the burning building would have been visible for miles.

"Like I said, try not to think about it," Karen had told them both, trying not to smile as the bagged bodies were borne off. "Things like this do happen occasionally in our line of work."

Becky had nodded and had kept her face expressionless, but she had already decided what she was going to do.

"Yeah, I guess so," she'd relied Karen, then had added, "but I can't stand the smoke, it's making me sick. I think I'll walk down to the church with dad so I'll have some fresh air."

And that was how she had accompanied her father back to the Joy of life church, with both Karen and her own monitoring familiar unaware of her true purpose in going to the church, because they were both too delighted by the death and destruction that they had just caused.

Because, yes, Karen actually had used Becky to do what she wanted.

And now, with tears streaming from her eyes, Becky told the pastor, "Sir, I have a confession to make..."

Pastor Fisher nodded soberly back at her. She understood that he was upset by the news of Mark's death which had preceded her here. And she knew he would be even more upset by what she had to tell him now.

And then she began telling Pastor Fisher the whole shocking story of her descent into Satanism.

CHAPTER 13

With an occasional glance at the fire burning in the near distance, Timothy Lowe worked happily on the roof of the church's administration building. Timothy was rather pleased by Mark Wilson's death, as he had long suspected him of having been Becky's lover at the time she'd had her accident.

"Well, she's killed the damned Christian fool now," he said, hammering at a shingle. "And I gotta say it sure is good riddance to bad rubbish. The less Christians in the world, the better."

Timothy glanced once more at the smoke rising into the sky, sniffed the air and imagined he could smell roasting bodies, and then resumed fixing the leak in the counseling room roof which Connie Davies had informed him of yesterday.

And then suddenly, like magic, Karen was up there on the roof with Timothy.

Timothy, who was balanced on the slanted roof shingles, almost lost his footing when Karen appeared above him, sitting on the ridge of the roof.

Once Timothy had regained his balance and had gotten over his shock, he realized that Karen was extremely angry about something. He also saw that she wasn't really there with him but was actually a projection—her body semitransparent as a ghost.

"What's the matter?" he asked in confusion.

"Your daughter has chosen to betray us," Karen informed him in a cold voice.

Timothy gaped at her and then shook his head. "Becky? Hell no, you must be mistaken. My Becky would never do that. Not after everything Satan has done for her."

"She's weak," Karen said. "Unfortunately for *you*, she has had a change of heart and is downstairs with the pastor right now, spilling the beans to him."

Timothy was silent while processing this. But then his mind latched on to a particular phrase of hers, and fright suddenly filled him:

"Er, Karen, what do you mean by 'unfortunately for me?' " he asked.

Karen smiled but her voice was cold and merciless. "Remember how Bill and I warned you last night that Satan doesn't tolerate repeated failures? And that he sometimes needs a scapegoat?" She shrugged. "Well, I'm sorry, old man, but in this case, you have been chosen as the scapegoat."

"But...but..." All that Timothy Lowe could think as the projection of Karen faded and the air around him filled up with huge black birds, was how unfair the Devil was being to him. Here he was, a dedicated worshipper of Satan for less than a week, and he was about to be punished for something that he hadn't done and didn't even know was occurring.

Oh, Becky, you silly little fool! He thought desperately and then the birds attacked him en masse. They swarmed over Timothy as if he was a tasty worm, all pecking at him at the same time.

Old Timothy had no idea when he lost his balance on the roof, but suddenly he was falling backwards, and then he was airborne and, crazily, as if the birds had somehow lifted him up through the air, Timothy seemed to be much higher above the ground than the roof he had been standing on.

And then, he was falling from a great height and screaming to the Devil for mercy.

And finally, Timothy Lowe crashed to earth, breaking his neck and shattering all of his bones. And even before his body was fully dead, his soul was being sucked down to Hell, where the demons waited for him with expectant grins on their ghastly faces, impatient to begin their eternal torment of Timothy's immortal soul.

CHAPTER 14

Pastor Fisher had informed Josh and Connie that a church member, Mark Wilson, had just died in the fire down the street, and they were waiting to meet with him about this once he got through counselling Becky Lowe, who happened to be the dead man's neighbor.

In fact, the pastoral trio had been about to begin their conference when Becky had arrived, but she had looked so distraught about her neighbor's grisly passing that Pastor Fisher had decided to attend to her first.

And this is why Josh and Connie were both seated in their office when the racket began.

"Oh, dear Lord Jesus!" Connie gasped, sticking her fingers in her ears. "Don't those birds ever stop? One would think that they hated God or something!"

Josh had been thinking exactly the same thing.

Although since Pastor Fisher had made it clear that under no circumstances would he permit them to either shoot or trap or poison the black birds the young couple had abducted a 'grin and bear' it policy towards the church's avian persecutors, this afternoon's racket had a special note to it. It sounded as if an entire flock of the birds—maybe the entirety of the species in the town—were fighting over something up on the roof.

"Hey, isn't that over where brother Timothy is working?" Josh finally asked after locating the source of the noise, to which Connie nodded.

And then the horrendous racket was replaced by empty silence, a lack of sound which was quickly filled by loud screaming that seemed to begin very high up in the air and then drop closer to the ground. And next came a horrible sickening thud a short distance away.

"Oh, my God, no!" Connie yelped into the scary silence that followed. And then both she and her husband were up on their feet and were running out of the office.

Connie took just one look at the mess that had been Timothy Lowe and then turned away and buried her face in her husband's chest, weeping for all she was worth.

Josh was struck speechless by the sight of the dead man's remains.

He had never seen such a mangled corpse before. Timothy's body was horribly contorted and there was hopeless look on his bloody face.

Wow, Josh thought, *he looks like he's gone to Hell!*

Josh groaned. Here he'd been, thanking the Lord that today he and Connie hadn't been plagued with silly arguments again, and now this happens...

Then a door opened behind them and they heard the sound of running feet.

It was Becky Lowe. With a loud shriek, Becky flung herself down on top of her father's bleeding corpse. "Oh, daddy, no!" she wept on his body. "Not you too! I didn't mean it! I didn't know what I was doing!"

Pastor Fisher arrived beside the corpse then, looking very troubled. Connie was still pressed hard against Josh's chest, but now, apparently feeling strong enough to look at the body, she pulled away from him and wiped tears from her eyes.

"Has anyone dialed 911 yet?" she asked.

Pastor Fisher shook his head. "Not unless you two have. Becky and I had no idea what the commotion outside was about."

"I'll do it then," Connie said, starting to turn around. "I'll get my phone from the office."

"Take Becky with you," Pastor Fisher told her. "Make her lie down on the couch in my office. Or better still, take her over to Madge in the parsonage."

It took some doing to prise Becky off of her father's corpse. She only let go of him when both Josh and Pastor Fisher took firm hold of her shoulders and pulled her away.

As Becky staggered back in their arms, Josh caught a glimpse of something bright on her chest. He paid it more attention; it was a black bird-shaped amulet.

Despite the serious situation now confronting them, Becky's amulet struck Josh as not exactly being 'Christian-friendly' jewelry. It seemed more like something a devil worshipper would wear.

What is she doing wearing this?

As Connie led the inconsolable young woman away, Josh realized that her amulet reminded him of the black birds. He turned and stared up at the roof where Timothy had been working. There were about twenty birds up there, lined up on the ridge of the roof.

"I think the birds caused his fall," he told Pastor Fisher.

But the pastor was staring out into the distance, where a thin stream of smoke still rose from Mark Wilson's razed residence, and apparently didn't hear Josh's statement.

"This is a terrible day," Pastor Fisher said. "Two deaths—two of our dedicated church members dying on the same afternoon. Oh, my dear Lord, I just hope they're not connected."

Josh considered repeating his statement that he thought the birds were responsible for Timothy's death, but then something about the corpse caught his attention.

The pastor was still staring out at the waning plume of smoke in the near-distance. Josh knelt beside the corpse and looked more closely.

Yes, it's exactly the same one. Timothy Lowe was wearing a similar black amulet to Becky's. The old man's fall had knocked the amulet out of the neckline of the plaid shirt beneath his faded work coveralls. There was very little blood on the amulet and its chain had snapped, so Josh picked it up. Pastor Fisher was still staring out into space when Josh straightened up again, so he slipped the amulet into his pocket.

They could discuss it later.

He stood beside the pastor, also staring into the distance, waiting for the authorities to come for the dead man. There could be no doubt that this was an accident, just as there was no doubt either about Mark Wilson's death being accidental.

But still, turning from staring at the smoke rising from the burnt residence ahead of him and then glancing back at Timothy's Lowe's corpse and then looking up again at the row of black avian sentinels, Josh felt chilled to his bones.

Lord God, he prayed, *I know this is crazy, but why do I get the feeling that all these birds knew exactly what they were doing when they made the old guy fall?*

And then, a memory coming to his mind, he asked, "Pastor, do you have any idea what Becky meant when she said that she didn't mean it, that she didn't know what she was doing?"

Pastor Fisher nodded his head glumly. "Yes, unfortunately I do. She hadn't told me too much though before the commotion out here began, and neither of us could concentrate after that."

Connie came out of the pastor's office then with a sheet to cover the body.

"She's a bit better," she told the two men. "She's the one who asked me to cover up the corpse."

Josh took the sheet from her and covered the dead man with it.

"I'm worried, pastor," Connie said when the body had been obscured from view.

"What worries you, sister?" the pastor asked kindly. "Yes, I know that today has been a very trying one, but our Lord Jesus gives us the victory in spite of all these setbacks." He smiled sadly at her. "Try to view it this way, sister Connie—that two of the Lord's faithful soldiers have been called back home."

"That's my point exactly, sir," Connie said. "You've already filled us in on the grievous spiritual attacks that this parish has been enduring over the years and how ever other church in this town has shut down one after another. And now..." she gestured helplessly down at the covered man, "now I just can't help wondering if this isn't the next phase of the Devil's assault against our church. Does he intend to begin picking us off one by one until there's no one left here to worship God?"

The pastor looked alarmed. "God forbid, sister Connie. Surely it won't ever come to that! Our Lord Jesus said, 'I will build my church and the gates of Hell will not prevail against it.' Oh yes, it has always been like this, right from the times of the first apostles: the church of Jesus Christ has always suffered intense attacks, both physical and spiritual. But no matter what the Devil has attempted, each time our Lord shows His glory and the forces of darkness are put to flight before His divine power and the Church rises stronger from the flames of the fire that was intended to burn it down."

A loud anguished cry came from the pastor's office. "Oh, no! Daddy, no!"

Connie looked at the two men in alarm. "I'll better go stay with Becky again and ensure that she doesn't harm herself."

The pastor nodded and she hurried off. In the distance Josh heard sirens approaching.

CHAPTER 15

After Timothy Lowe's body had been collected by the ambulance, Josh, Connie and Pastor Fisher retired to the pastor's office for a conference.

"This has been a horribly stressful day for all of us," Pastor Fisher stated. "And it looks to become even more so in a little while. Other than for sister Juanita, no one else has yet been informed of the deaths."

Sister Juanita was a nurse. When Becky had become unmanageable, the pastor's wife had phoned her and requested that she come over to the parsonage to sedate Becky. Becky was now asleep in one of the parsonage's guest rooms.

"She clearly can't go home now," sister Juanita had explained. "One sight of that burnt house next door and she'll likely freak out again."

Sister Juanita was over in the parsonage now, keeping an eye on Becky.

"She was saying some really weird stuff when we were alone," Connie told Josh and the pastor after they had said a prayer to invite God to oversee the meeting. "She seems to think she's in some way responsible for her father's death."

Josh looked at the pastor. "Sir, you said she told you some things too."

"Yes, she claimed that both she and her father had made a deal with the Devil for her healing," Pastor

Fisher said. "Of course, that's pure nonsense. We all know that God healed her, but..."

But as the pastor dismissed Becky's confession, Josh remembered the weird feeling he'd had when Becky had gotten her miracle, that feeling that something had been very 'off' about it.

"...I mean, why would Satan give his sworn enemy, our Lord Jesus, credit for a healing? It makes no sense at all."

"I agree with that," Connie said, then she looked over at Josh. "Darling, what's the matter?"

"Oh, I just remembered I had this on me," Josh said, pulling the black bird amulet out of his pocket and placing it on the pastor's office desk. "Brother Timothy was wearing it when he died."

"I don't see what..." the pastor began; but then his eyes narrowed. "Hey, what is going on here? This pendant looks like one of those annoying birds that are everywhere!"

He looked at Josh in surprise. Josh nodded back.

"Becky is wearing a necklace exactly like this one!" Connie exclaimed. "I remember it because sister Juanita said it looked really creepy."

"Brethren, I believe we need to pray about this right now," Pastor Fisher said grimly.

They bent their heads and the pastor led them: "Our dear Lord and Almighty Father, please help us now as the gates of Hell have once more rallied their evil forces against this little church. Almighty God, in the name of Jesus, we ask you to..."

Josh prayed along with the pastor, and as he did so, deep in his heart he kept hearing the single word 'deliverance' repeated: "Deliverance...deliverance... deliverance..." It was a simple instruction, and Josh knew he wasn't mishearing it.

"...in Jesus' name, amen," Pastor Fisher finished the prayer.

Josh told the others what the Holy Spirit had revealed to him. "I think that to get to the root of all this we need to exorcise sister Becky," he said.

Connie instantly nodded. "I have the same feeling."

Pastor Fisher though looked unsure. "Exorcisms can be very dangerous. Two deaths in one day are bad enough, but what happens if something goes awry and Becky dies on us also? Remember that neither brother Mark's nor Timothy's deaths can be blamed on the church—one occurred at his home, the other occurred during a routine repair job..." He paused and gazed at them both seriously. "But if anything goes wrong during our exorcism of sister Becky...at the very least it'll be a double tragedy in the same family, and on the same day."

"I'm sorry to disagree, sir," Josh said firmly, picking up the bird amulet and swinging it so that the pastor got his point. "But I don't think we've a choice now. I clearly heard the Spirit of God speaking to me, and he was very clear that he wants us to conduct deliverance—an exorcism—on sister Becky."

The pastor looked pained. Josh shared his concerns, but he honestly also felt that there was nothing they could do but follow God's instructions on this matter.

"If we don't at least *try* to exorcise her, with the way she's ranting, she might run mad," Connie pointed out, "and whatever is possessing her might ultimately destroy her."

Pastor Fisher still clearly disliked the idea. But he just as clearly also saw that they had no choice in the matter.

Finally, the pastor sighed. "Okay, we'll hold the exorcism after tonight's Bible study service," he said quietly. "That way there'll be no interruptions." Then he sighed even louder. "And folks will soon start arriving for the Bible study. I really don't look forward to telling them about these two deaths."

CHAPTER 16

"An exorcism, huh?" Bill Houston said, squinting at the tiny figures visible in his sister's crystal ball. None of those he was watching had a clue that one of the black birds was perched on the windowsill of the pastor's office and was keeping a close eye on them.

Karen, who was poised over the crystal ball with her hands outstretched, frowned. "We'll just have to break things up," she said. "We've already lost Timothy. Losing Becky too would be completely unacceptable. There's no point killing her as well. The Black Circle is trying to recruit followers in this stupid town, not to kill everyone. Her father was old and expendable; she's young and still very useful to us."

"She's already begun talking," Bill pointed out, taking a sip from his can of beer. "She'll confess everything to the church."

"She'll only confess if we let her," Karen corrected him, moving away from the crystal ball to sit by Bill's side. "What we need for little Becky is a demonstration of power that'll scare her to our side for good."

Bill slurped some beer. "What do you have in mind?"

Karen pointed to the crystal ball in which, unaware that their secret plans were out in the open to their enemies, the conference continued.

"Oh, we'll let the Christians conduct their little exorcism," Karen said mockingly. "But we'll make it such a bloody spectacle that no one in that damned church will ever attempt one again."

CHAPTER 17

"You look really bothered about something," Josh told Connie after they'd left the pastor's office and were walking to the church auditorium. "Was there something else that you sensed about Becky's case?"

Connie told Josh what was on her mind:

"Bill and Karen are here in Wickenburg," she said. "I just felt it while we were praying; but for some reason I didn't feel like telling the pastor about them."

"Oh, my God," Josh said on hearing the names of his ex-girlfriend and her brother mentioned. "Not those two again."

Connie nodded. "And, from what I felt the Holy Spirit was telling me, the pair of them are somehow directly involved in Becky's case."

Josh looked skyward. "Oh, Lord Jesus, help us."

CHAPTER 18

At 10 p.m. that night Bill and Karen locked the door of their house and stood in their driveway.

"That was a job well done," Bill congratulated his sister, pointing to Mark Wilson's gutted house. "I hated how he became a dedicated Christian again once his wife died."

"Time to go," Karen told him, tugging on his sleeve. "I sense that the exorcism is about to begin."

Bill nodded.

And then both siblings transformed themselves into black birds and flew off down their street towards the Joy of Life church. And as they went, streams of other black birds from all across Wickenburg flocked through the air and joined them, until by the time they'd reached the church and its unsuspecting ministers, the birds were almost a hundred in number, all of them hungry and thirsty for the flesh and blood of Christians.

Under the cover of the night, these birds settled over the church in an evil black cloud.

The battle lines had been drawn.

CHAPTER 19

The deliverance/exorcism of Becky Lowe was conducted in the living room of the church parsonage. Becky had by now woken up from her drugged sleep, but still seemed a little dazed.

"She'll be like this for a couple of hours longer," sister Juanita had informed the pastor before leaving for home after the church service. Josh and Connie would have loved for sister Juanita to have been present for the deliverance prayers, but she had to get back to her husband and children.

So now, except for Becky and the quartet of exorcists—the Fishers and the Davieses—the church grounds were empty.

Becky now sat in one of the living room armchairs. Madge Fisher had suggested that maybe they should restrain her in some way, but her husband had told everyone it wasn't necessary.

"It sounds like it's going to rain," Connie said on hearing a rumbling noise begin outside.

Josh listened too. There had been a slight drizzle during the church service, and the air blowing into the parsonage smelled clean and fresh.

This doesn't sound like rain, Josh thought. *It sounds almost like the beating wings of a large flock of birds.*

The thought disturbed him, but on stepping up to the living room windows and looking out through them, he saw no sign of any birds. He squinted up at the black heavens looking for them.

"Please, brother Josh, don't let anything distract you now. It's time to pray for our sister Becky," Pastor Fisher said.

Still bothered by the thick murmuring noise outside, that sound like the beating of a hundred unseen wings, Josh tried to concentrate on the task they were here for.

I'm the one who insisted on us doing this, he thought. *The pastor is right—I can't let myself be distracted.*

Bibles in hand and with Pastor Fisher slightly in front of the others, the four of them stood facing the seated woman.

"Now, sister Rebecca, do you renounce Satan and all of his works? Do you fully accept the lordship of Jesus Christ?"

Becky never answered the pastor's question, because at the moment she opened her mouth to do so, that ominous rumbling noise which had been growing steadily louder over the past minute suddenly exploded into a thunderous pattering on the roof of the parsonage.

"It's the birds," Connie exclaimed. "Lord Jesus, what do they want now?"

"Ignore them," Pastor Fisher instructed as the noise continued to increase in volume, now accompanied by the clear sound of flapping wings. Then he looked once more at Becky. "I insist that you answer me, sister. Do you desire the Lord's deliverance from the powers of—"

But Becky's face suddenly twisted up in a snarl and she launched herself out of the chair at the pastor, with her nails hooked into claws to scratch his face.

Pastor Fisher got out of the way just in time. While yelling, "In the name of Jesus!" Josh rushed past him and knocked Becky back down into the armchair.

But she was up again in an instant, flinging Josh aside as if he weighed nothing at all.

She stood there in the middle of the room snarling like a beast.

Josh and Connie had never seen anything like this before: Becky's eyes had now turned completely black, her skin had taken on a purple tinge with bulging black veins running across its surface, and streams of saliva poured from her mouth.

But the biggest shock came when she spoke. The voice that proceeded from between her lips was a masculine one, gutturally deep and hash in timbre.

"This one is mine!" it thundered, so loud that it easily cut through the noise the birds were making outside. "She has pledged herself to me and you cannot have her back!"

"Demon, I rebuke you in the name of Jesus!" Pastor Fisher thundered in return. "This one belongs to Jesus! Be gone from her!"

In response, the demon-possessed woman laughed. "No, she is mine! Mine forever!"

"Come out of her, you foul spirit!" Josh ordered.

But instead, Becky lunged at Madge Fisher. Before the others could intervene, she picked Madge up and flung her across the living room. Madge hit the far wall, bounced off of it, and crashed down behind the couch.

"NOOO!" her husband yelled, turning to look at where she had fallen out of sight.

"I'm fine!" Madge called out weakly from behind the couch. Then they saw her brown hair start to appear above the couch's backrest.

Outside, the black birds were squawking and cawing like mad. The sound filled everyone's heads, until Josh and Connie both thought they were going insane from it. The current moment seemed something to endure, not something that could be overcome by mere statements of one's faith in God.

Josh looked down at the Bible he was clutching. Despite his trust in its truths, the holy book suddenly seemed very inadequate to the demands of this situation.

Madge Fisher's head finally appeared completely from behind the couch. She had a bleeding cut across her forehead. She waved at them to show that she was okay and then sunk back out of sight again.

But this distraction almost cost Pastor Fisher dearly. Because now, Becky swung around, grabbed up a large screwdriver that had been left on the coffee table, and swung it at the pastor's neck.

Josh interceded just in time. He flung himself between the possessed woman and the pastor, shoving Pastor Fisher out of the way.

However, Josh paid for his heroism: the screwdriver stabbed deep into his upper arm, and he staggered back howling in pain, while 'Becky' clutched the bloody screwdriver in her hand and laughed uproariously.

"Hahaha! You silly Christians are so weak and so is your pathetic God! I'll teach you all a lesson tonight that you'll never forget!"

By now the birds' unearthly noise had risen to a crescendo. The noise was a strident chorus of avian displeasure that seemed to exist everywhere at once around them. The uproar made prayer seem impossible to Josh.

Gripping his arm to stop the bleeding, Josh looked over at his wife, who stared back at him with scared eyes. He understood her dilemma: during their time as preachers neither of them had ever come up against something like this before. The demons they had encountered had been much simpler to deal with.

But, staring at Becky Lowe, who now looked as if she had been painted purple and black, whose eyes were black as coal, and who was clawing at the air with her left-hand fingers, stabbing the air with the screwdriver held in her right hand, and swaying back and forth while balanced on her toes, Josh felt momentarily outclassed.

Connie took a step towards him but he waved her back. He didn't want her close to the danger that Becky was now.

"I'm okay!" he shouted to her over the birds' noise which had now stabilized at an incredibly loud volume; louder than bombs even, was how it sounded.

Pastor Fisher was out cold on the floor, knocked unconscious by his fall when Josh shoved him out of the way of the demon's attack; and the pastor's wife was still out of sight somewhere behind the couch.

Josh realized that it was up to himself and Connie to handle matters now. And he wasn't sure he knew what to do.

"Oh, Mighty God, what do we do now?" he prayed silently, desperately focusing his thoughts through the noise.

"Throw your Bible at her," replied the quiet voice of the Holy Spirit.

"Yes, Lord, thank you," Josh said, and immediately flung his Bible at Becky, who seemed to be about to launch herself at the unconscious pastor again to stab him with her screwdriver.

Becky howled in rage when the Bible hit her. For a moment she seemed to expand as if exploding, but then she staggered backwards and finally slumped back down into the armchair she had originally been sitting in.

Most importantly, her body instantly lost its unnatural purple color, and her eyes returned to their normal shade of pale green.

She stared at them weakly from the armchair, no longer having sufficient strength to rise, and barely able to speak.

"Help me!" she whispered in an agonized voice, with tears streaming down her cheeks. "I really don't want to be like this anymore. I want Jesus back again. Please forgive me, Lord Jesus. I'm truly sorry for everything I've done."

It was then that Josh realized that the birds had stop making their awful din. The world around them was completely silent.

Now thoroughly emboldened and confident of their victory in Jesus, Josh and Connie stepped up close to Becky.

"You demonic spirits oppressing sister Becky, come out of her right now in Jesus' mighty name."

On that spiritual command Becky fell back into the chair with her eyes shut as if she was unconscious. Then her mouth yawned open and a stream of birds—these ones little semitransparent black birds that seemed half liquid, as if they were melting into one another—flew out of her mouth.

Of the fact that these tiny creatures exiting Becky's mouth were Evil incarnate there was no doubt at all in the mind of the young exorcist couple.

"Jesus!" Connie gasped in shock as the tiny birds circled once around the room above their heads and then vanished through the ceiling.

Then she and her husband got down on their knees on the floor of the parsonage living room and began singing songs of praise and glory to God Almighty.

After a while Madge Fisher crawled out from behind the couch and went to her husband's side, where she laid her head on his prone body and praised God along with the others.

And then, suddenly, bright lights filled the heavens over the little church.

CHAPTER 20

Outside the church parsonage dead birds rained down like hailstones. As the Christians in the pastor's house praised God, the glory of God became visible in the clouds over the little town of Wickenburg and the powers of Evil had no reply to it.

Bolts of crystal-clear light struck the parsonage roof like a fireworks display. It was a terrifying display of God's power and the surviving black birds scattered in every direction, with those that weren't fast enough succumbing to the bolts of light and joining their dead fellows on the ground.

"We need to get out of here fast!" Bill squawked at his sister.

But just as the transformed brother and sister took flight, a bolt of God's holy lightning struck Bill.

Being human, however, and not a true bird, Bill managed to keep flying, although he grew weaker with each wing beat. He and Karen reached their bungalow safely, and both alighted safely onto their driveway, but then while Karen transformed back to her normal human form without any difficulty, the black bird that had been Bill Houston emitted a weak croak of agony and toppled over onto its side.

Oh no! Karen thought desperately, bending down and scooping up the bird, while in the distance the fireworks-like display of God's immense glory continued across the roofs of the Joy of Life church's buildings.

Karen ran into the house to see what could be done for her brother, but soon gave up in frustration; she had seen this before, more than once.

Nothing could be done for the moment; Bill was stuck in a state of unconsciousness and transformed stasis for the time being. He would remain a bird for the foreseeable future until Karen could figure out the proper way to reverse him back to normal.

Once she understood the depths of their defeat, Karen walked angrily back outside to her driveway and shook her fist at the Joy of life Church.

Over there, the glorious aerial lightshow was now ending and leaving the night as dark as it had been before Becky's exorcism commenced.

Karen glared at the church and vowed to get revenge on the Christians for what they had done to her brother.

"I will destroy you, all of you, if it is the last thing I ever do in my life."

CHAPTER 21

"Oh, praise the Lord—our God really showed himself glorious last night," Pastor Fisher proclaimed with great enthusiasm the next morning, when they all stepped out of the parsonage and saw the number of dead birds in the church compound.

All of them, that is, except Becky Lowe, whom, now that the evil spirits had gone out of her, could no longer walk.

But Becky didn't mind being crippled again, she'd said.

"I'm simply delighted to be back in the Lord's fold, back beneath the saving grace of the blood of Jesus." She'd wept, tears rolling down her cheeks. "Oh, my God, you have no idea what it was like doing those horrible things to innocent people!"

They had been shocked when she'd told them everything she and her father had done using the birds, how deep into Satanism they'd sunk in such a short time.

Josh and Connie were equally shocked by her confirmation that their old adversaries Bill and Karen Houston were the masterminds behind everything that had recently been going wrong at the Joy of life church.

"They told me to pretend that it was God who'd healed me not the Devil," Becky had said.

"Oh yes, God really gave us the victory," Josh agreed with the pastor, and then, while wincing from the pain in his now bandaged arm, he and Connie walked around the parsonage counting the number of dead birds scattered everywhere.

"That makes at least fifty birds," Josh said as they returned around the side of the building and headed back toward the pastor and his wife.

Connie pointed up at the roof. "Wow, and that's not counting all those that didn't fall to the ground. We're going to need to get someone to bring them all down from the roof or else they'll soon start stinking."

Josh nodded, but didn't say anything. He was sadly remembering Becky's father Timothy, and the horrifying hell-bound expression that the old man had had on his face when he died.

"Now, sir, do you agree with me that these birds are a nuisance, something we need to get an exterminator to tackle?" Josh asked Pastor Fisher.

Josh was certain that this time he would get a positive reply to his suggestion that they trap and kill the black birds.

But once more Pastor Fisher refused to agree with him. "There's no more need to kill them ourselves now," he said. "The Lord Almighty has already done the job for us." The pastor gestured around at the large feathered bodies strewn everywhere. "And what a great extermination job our Lord has done. One would almost think he was providing flesh for us to eat just like he did for the Children of Israel in the desert."

And then he began laughing. After a few seconds Josh and Connie and the pastor's wife burst into laughter too.

The End

ABOUT THE AUTHOR

Gary Lee Vincent was born in Clarksburg, West Virginia and is an accomplished author, musician, actor, producer, director and entrepreneur. In 2010, his horror novel *Darkened Hills* was selected as 2010 Book of the Year winner by *Foreword Reviews Magazine* and became the pilot novel for *DARKENED - THE WEST VIRGINIA VAMPIRE SERIES*, that encompasses the novels *Darkened Hills, Darkened Hollows, Darkened Waters, Darkened Souls, Darkened Minds* and *Darkened Destinies.* He has also authored the bizarro thriller *Passageway,* a tribute to H.P. Lovecraft.

Gary co-authored the novel *Belly Timber* with John Russo, Solon Tsangaras, Dustin Kay and Ken Wallace, and co-authored the novel *Attack of the Melonheads* with Bob Gray and Solon Tsangaras.

As an actor, Gary has appeared in over seventy feature films and multiple television series, including *House of Cards*, *Mindhunter*, *The Walking Dead*, and *Stranger Things*.

As a director, Gary got his directorial debut with *A Promise to Astrid.* He has also directed the films *Desk Clerk*, *Dispatched*, *Midnight, Godsend,* and *Strange Friends.*

Also in Burning Bulb Publishing Christian Fantasy:

STRANGE FRIENDS

GARY LEE VINCENT

PROVE YOUR LOVE

THE BLACK CIRCLE CHRONICLES - BOOK 1

GARY LEE VINCENT

GODSEND

RICH BOTTLES JR.

Made in the USA
Columbia, SC
27 September 2022

67725014R00057